Winston's Fire

by Nathan Chips

BookSolid Press

Imprint of Transpersonal Publishing, AHU.LLC
P.O. Box 7220, Kill Devil Hills, NC 27948
www.TranspersonalPublishing.Com

Orders:
Wholesale—www.TranspersonalPublishing.com
Retail—www.Holistictree.com

Illustrations by Katie Wahl

First printing, first edition: May, 2006

ISBN 1-929661-23-1 (soft cover edition)

All Transpersonal Publishing titles, imprints, and distributed lines are available at special quantity discounts for bulk purchases for sales promotions, premiums, fund-raising, and educational or institutional use. Special book excerpts or customized printings can also be created to fit specific needs.

For details, contact the Publisher at
www.TranspersonalPublishing.com or 800-296-MIND.

Printed in the India
10 9 8 7 6 5 4 3 2 1

Once upon a time, there lived a happy squirrel.

This happy squirrel's name was Winston.

Winston lived on Cherry Lane.

One day, when Winston woke up he said, "Mom can I go into town today ?"

"No," said mother, "You're going to start going to school today."

"SCHOOL! Do I have to?"

"Yes, after all, you're five whole years old."

"But..." Winston continued, "I don't want to mom. I'm scared."

"I'm sure once you get used to it, Winston, you'll love it, and forget all about being scared," said mother.

So they got in the car and drove up to the new school.

"Here we are," said mother.

As they walked up to the front doors of the school, Winston was very nervous.

Then when they went inside, Winston took a look around and saw that all of the other kids were scared too.

A kid named Tommy came up to him and said, "Hi. What's your name?"

"Winston," he said.

"My name is Tommy; I'm a penguin."

The rest of the day flew by like a breeze.

Winston was having so much fun that he forgot all about being scared.

In fact, the end of the day came so quickly that when Winston's mother came to pick him up, Winston didn't want to go home.

Then Winston said good bye
to his new friend Tommy and
went home looking forward
to tomorrow.

THE END

Nathan Chips was 14 years old when he wrote this book, the first of a collection of books geared toward the first-time experiences of children. Though he recognizes the value of similar books he was exposed to as a young child, his work is purely original.

Nathan lived in the mountains of Virginia when he created Winston's First Day of School, but now resides in Outer Banks, North Carolina, where he attends high school, enjoys surfing, fishing, boating, playing drums, and other teen activities.

Nathan travels for book signings in the United States and abroad and currently works for the independent press that published this book. His future plans include writing more books and continuing a career in the literary and publishing fields upon graduating from college.